ROLLY PASILAN

The Wolf Who Steals My Heart

Contents

1 Chapter 1 — 1
2 Chapter 2 — 10
3 Chapter 3 — 20
4 Chapter 4 — 26
5 Love Poems — 36
6 The Halfling — 40

1

Chapter 1

Every time I pass by a school, it gives me a feeling of being a puppy; wherever her canine parent goes, she goes with him.

It *is* June again, a time to go back to school. I sigh knowing that the school I am gazing at will be my third school for my high school life. I swear in Lapu-Lapu's name; this is my third time. I feel it's some kind of hassle and not a pleasure to see and meet new people—nosy and noisy classmates, strict or soft-spoken teachers, a terrifying principal, etc. I find it uncomfortable to adjust to a new environment every time we transfer to another place.

I know you understand me if I say that I dislike my dad—not that I dislike him as a person, but I dislike his job. I don't know why, on earth, dad chose to be a construction worker. Why not a lawyer, a doctor, or a teacher?

"Why construction worker, Dad?" I ask him while his eyes are fixed on the road, driving. I want to sit at the back where I can freely move my legs, but I don't want to look like a maleficent girl, making her dad look like a Hired. Grab. Driver.

"Everly, this is a noble job. Imagine a world without people like me. There will be no towering buildings, houses, bridges, and... schools." Dad emphasizes the last word, for he knows that I like studying very much. His tone is melodramatic, as if he could get a Metro Manila Film Festival Best Actor nomination for his speech. Seriously, he's a cool, jolly person. Rarely does he get angry at me or other people. And every time I ask that question of him, I get the same response over and over with the same tone. I always want to break into laughter every time he does it. That's Tom Wolfe, a muscular man with an apple-shaped face and a well-trimmed beard who happens to be my great father; he prefers to be called "Dad" rather than "Papa" or "*Tatay*." If I have a choice, I'll call him "Papi."

"And let me add, your Dad got promoted to assistant fore-man."

"Congratulations, Dad! I'm proud of you."

Speaking of studying, thanks to mom, I get her drive to study. That's what Granny Audrey, my mom's mother, always tells me. But it's so unthinkable that she passed away when she gave birth to me. Am I the cause of her death? Sometimes, in my solitary moments, I question God. Why, Lord? Why her? Why not me?

When I ask my dad about her looks, he'll always say, "You look like your Mom. Simply beautiful!"

Uh. I can't say thank you enough to dad. He has been both a MoDa (mom and dad) to me. He has been a good provider to the family, from the food he brings to the table to the clothes I wear.

Dad *is* making a left turn onto a road where towering acacia and palm trees proudly stand. When I open the window, the gentle breeze smooches my skin and playfully messes my shoulder-length brown hair, and the sweet aroma of freshly harvested corn scents the air.

As I'm enjoying the moment, a young man in a black shirt

gazes at me from a distance. I take a few glances at him to see his face, but his hood somehow covers half of his face. Maybe he intentionally does it so I can't see him, and I swear in Christ's name he keeps staring at me. Believe me, I catch him when a strong gust of wind blows his hood off. Does he own the STARING BUSINESS, or does he have a FRANCHISE of it?

I close the window, take my cellphone out of my jeans pocket, and pretend that I don't notice him. I open my social media account and am about to post an Instagrammable photo I took an hour ago of the majestic scenery of the place when the car suddenly stops. I jerk. Thanks to the seat belt. My face doesn't hit the glass frame, or the frame will shatter into a hundred fragments. *Jeez.*

"Goodness gracious me," I say with raised brows. "W-w-what's wrong, Dad?" My voice seems to falter.

"Have you seen that?" Dad's eyes widen as if they would pop out from his eyelids.

"What?"

"A huge dog is crossing the way."

"I don't see it, Dad." I shrug.

"I swear it. It's huge, as in a huge dog."

"Really? Look, Dad, this is a town covered with trees. A stray dog is not peculiar to see."

"Unless it is as huge as the one I see, I swear it, honey."

"Okay, I believe you then." I pat his shoulder to give him confirmation that I believe in him. If my dad says it, it's true. I trust him. He's telling the truth. Just like me, I use that expression to convince anybody that what I'm saying is the truth and nothing but the truth. If there is something I get from my dad, it's his honesty and his "I SWEAR IT" expression.

Dad starts the car, yet the engine doesn't roar. I see disbelief in his eyes.

"Not this time. Common!" My dad starts again, and it creates some squeaky sounds. He tries it a few times, but his moves seem futile. Shaking his head, he gets out and checks the front and calls my name.

"Everly, call your Granny. Tell her we might be late for lunch, but assure her that we're near her place. I'll fix this."

"Yes, Dad." I search for Granny's number in my contact list and dial it while my dad goes to the trunk and comes back with his toolbox. Granny and I talk over the phone for a couple of minutes when I hear a manly voice behind our car.

"Need help?"

"Hell yeah," Dad replies.

I tell Granny to hang on, whirl around, and see the man with a hood. He nears the front and checks the car.

"It's a spark plug. Don't worry; it will be fixed in less than ten minutes.

"Thanks, man."

Holy Molly. He's yummy. I'm squirting, baby. Joke.

"Gross. You're only sixteen, girl," my inner goddess, witch, or whatever reminds me.

The young man nods, flashing his dimples with certainty. I try to survey his appearance as if I'm a spy, remembering every detail of his well-chiseled face, which resembles that of a Korean superstar, Kim Soo-hyun. He's devilishly delicious. His piercing aquamarine eyes speak a thousand tales of happiness as they meet my hazelnuts. However, looks can be deceiving. If he's a serial killer, I may as well carve his appearance in my mind so I can vividly sketch or give details to the cop in case we escape. I must dial the police hotline number if he makes a wrong move. But Christ, it can't be denied the man stands like a demigod. His lean yet muscular build will make any young lady drool or swoon over him if he embraces her. *Gosh.*

I shift my attention to my phone... yeah, my phone. My granny is still on the line. I smack my palm against my forehead for being oblivious. This isn't me. I have a retentive memory. Is it because of him? Is it because of his stare? *No, nobody can do this to me... ever.*

I apologize to Granny, and we keep talking.

Thank God! After several light years, my dad clambers into the car.

"He's a nice guy."

"I thought he was a serial killer, Dad."

"Well, that's the effect of watching too many mystery and suspense movies."

I brush it off. "I guess."

The man signals to start the car, and by the time my dad does, the engine roars to life again, and oh boy, he nears me.

Holy snake. I'm swooning. He moves to the side of the car where I'm sitting.

"*ASSUMING... in all caps,*" my inner witch mutters, her hands planted on her hips.

Dad makes a thumbs-up sign while he gestures a salute, half-smiling. I can see his figure in the side mirror as we leave him on the road.

"Do you like him?"

"Hell no, Dad!" I say, pouting my lips. "What made you say so?"

"You keep glaring at him."

"I try to be a keen observer." *Dad, can't you pretend that you don't see anything?*

"You say so."

I pinch my dad while he messes with my hair... making it messier after the breeze has done so.

"My girl *is* now a lady. I think it's about time you'll admire someone or perhaps have one."

"Dad, in case you forget, I'm still sixteen."

"Hell yeah, you're sixteen, and you're thinking of squirting, baby." My inner witch strikes for the second time.

"Well, it's just admiration. Rarely do I see you with boys. Are you?"

"Dad, I'm not a lesbian. Well, there's nothing wrong with being one, but I'm not. I'm straight." *I'm Eve, not Steve, Dad.*

Dad shrugs. "Okay."

The car pulls to a stop at a Spanish-inspired house. My granny, in her early sixties, stands at the doorway. I clamber out of the car and shut the door. I sashay fast so I can come near her and give her a superpower hug, like I hug her tightly and move our bodies as if we were dancing. If there's any woman I have looked up to, it's my Granny. She's the epitome of beauty and substance. She speaks softly and never turns her back on someone in need. She tries to extend help to the needy as best she can, using the resources she has.

"Hi, Everly. I miss you so much. And welcome to Nivel Hills, Cebu City." Granny kisses me on the cheeks. Her cracked lips—maybe she has forgotten to use her lip balm for the past few months—speak of truth and virtue.

"I miss you too, Granny." I kiss her back and flash a saccharine smile.

It's a long exchange of pleasantries before we dash inside. The aroma of the food invites my nostrils to head to the kitchen. Different types of mouth-watering meals like pizza, rice cakes, *adobo*, *lechon*, and fruit salad with some fresh lettuce as its toppings catch my attention. I settle myself in a chair and whisper a prayer while Granny sits with stars in her eyes next to me. I take a plate and a spoon for my food. I feast on the pizza and the lettuce, and my mouth waters. Even though I eat a lot, I don't get fat. Thanks to my metabolism.

I sip a glass of fresh cucumber juice when my dad comes in; he pulls a chair for himself. I'm halfway finished when Granny asks me.

"So what caused your delay?"

I give Granny a sweet grin. "Something about the spark plug. Am I right, Dad?"

"Yeah. Faulty spark plug. The spark plug is faulty, as it may be, but there's still a spark... like someone I know who gets sparks for somebody." Dad's grinning at me.

There he goes again.

"Dad." I roll my eyes. "I know what you mean." I pout my lips in irritation. I don't know why my dad insists I like the guy, but maybe it's a man's intuition... sort of. Maybe that's how he perceives me when I gawk at his "newfound friend," but I don't know my feelings... yet. All I know is that I can't take my eyes off him. If it's admiration, so be it, but I want to make it clear: I'm not ready for it... not for now.

"Are you sure, baby girl?" My inner witch teases.

"Did you meet someone on the road?" Granny asks.

We both nod. Then my dad says it briskly. "He helps us fix my car."

"Good. Do you know his name?"

"Denver."

"Are you sure?" Granny's forehead crinkles.

"Unless I mishear it," Dad quips.

"Well, he's a nice guy," Granny says matter-of-factly.

"Do you know him, Granny?" I ask.

"I do... a little."

"Does he live near our place?"

"Yes, he does."

"By the way, how do you know him?" I ask. I can't understand why I become inquisitive about him as if I care about where he dwells.

"Go for it, my girl. Push it further. Solicit more information about him," Mr. Teaser Dad says.

"Dad, please stop it. I love investigative journalism, you know, documentaries about ordinary guys doing extraordinary things."

"Yes, I know," Dad says, chortling.

"Oh, never mind, Granny. You don't need to answer it. Hmm, can I go to my room now?"

"Of course, my dear, I'll bring you there."

I excuse myself from Mr. Teaser. Granny and I glide upstairs. She leads me to a room, in my mom's room when she was young. It's still cozy, spacious, and lovely. I think somebody stays there and maintains its beauty. I'm surprised to see my luggage beside the bed.

"Who brings it here, Granny?"

"My helper."

"I see. Granny, can I see Mom's photo album? I just want to have a glimpse of her." I plead in a sweet voice with puppy eyes so she can't refuse me. For my entire life, I've been content with my dad's story about her: her looks, her character, her strengths, and her flaws. Dad's tears streamed down his cheeks when he narrated their love story to me. But he made me promise that after it, there would be no questions about her. Dad didn't even show me my mom's photo because he didn't want me to live in the past. He wanted me to leave it behind and move on with optimism and cheerfulness. Dad's a realist. I don't question him about his decision, for I love and respect him very much.

Granny pulls something from a drawer. When she nears me, she hands me the thing I have wanted since childhood. We sit on the bed and flip through the transparent plastic as the photos of mom during her babyhood, childhood, and adolescent years abound on it. True enough, I look exactly like her when she was a teenager. I'm her carbon copy. My eyes sting as I flip through her photos. Granny caresses my back as I sob.

"It's okay, my dear. Crying is a sign of maturity, but don't cry a river, or else we'll get drowned here." Granny jokes, and I grin while tears well in my eyes.

2

Chapter 2

The first day is high. True to its word, students are high...as in hyperactive.

I'm gliding along the hallway when I see several students walk to and fro to say hi and hello to each other. Others are chit-chatting about the topics; hell, I care to know while some sit on the benches, standing along the corridors, chuckling.

It's still 7:50 in the morning, yet a lot of students have already crowded the school, excited to meet their friends, to share their family outings with them, and to discuss their two-month escapade.

Am I going to share with them that I woke up with long, black hair this morning? *Weird.* Even my dad noticed it, and I told him that I dye my hair and use extensions. I *lied.*

I can smell the earthy perfume of the newly trimmed grasses on the lawn, and their color is refreshing to the eyes. I continue walking until a young lady, who is probably my age, bumps me. She's chubby with hardly any neck and wears an extra-large pink blouse and skirt.

"I'm sorry. My bad." I try to sound apologetic with my eyes

looking like I don't know where to go. I don't want to mess up with someone on the first day, especially this chubby one.

"It's okay. Are you a newbie?" Ms. Chubby asks.

"Yeah, I don't know where my room is. I'm checking—"

"No problem." She muzzles. "9th grade?"

"10th grade."

"That sounds pretty cool. I'm in the 10th grade, too. I think we belong to the same section. I'm Stephanie."

"Glad to hear that. I'm Everly." I find comfort in her presence. I don't want to go to the principal's office or any teacher asking for his assistance to bring me to my room. I'm not a kid anymore, but I don't want to end the day sitting somewhere figuring out where my room is.

"Well, it's too early to go to our room. Our class starts at 8:20. So we still have twenty minutes to go to my place."

"Your place? Here in school?"

"Yes," Stephanie answers, grinning. "Trust me. Let's go."

I want to protest that I won't go with her, but she's way too bubbly to turn down. Besides, I can tell Steph's a nice girl and not a vampire. She's not going to tie me there, slash my neck, and drink my blood. *Oh, gosh!* This is what my dad has told me: the effect of watching too many mystery and fantasy movies. It sucks... really... sometimes.

She leads me to the back of the school, to a place under a mango tree. I can see a pathway leading to a dense forest, but I rest under the sturdy tree. The breeze is gentle and soothing, and I can sit under nature's shade on the green grasses all day long. A few leaves start to fall like confetti in the symphony of reds and oranges, while some sway to the music of the wind. Perhaps this is the perfect place to run if I have some melancholic moments.

"Nice place."

"Thanks. This is my fortress. I come here every time I can't endure their bullying of me."

"You're being bullied?" I inquire. I want to confirm if what I've heard is accurate. Given that I'm new, I might also be bullied. I want to get ready for my piece of the pie.

"Do I want to say it again? It seems you want me to sound like a broken CD player." Stephanie pouts and crosses her arms over her chest, giving the impression that she is disgusted. Her gesture causes me to laugh rather than get scared. "Just kidding."

"I know. Hmm, who bullies you?"

"I'm not allowed to mention their names."

"Why not? Why won't you report them to the teacher or the principal?"

"It's a waste of time," Stephanie quips, shaking her head. "I fight back against them. I was born to be a fighter, you know." Stephanie clinches her right fist to her left open palm.

"That's the spirit, girl."

"I bet you won't experience what I've gone through."

"You think so?"

"Hell yeah, because you're pretty and slender."

I chortle. "Thanks. I hope so."

"So, why do you study here?"

"Dad's doing. He's an assistant foreman. So every time he gets a new job in another city or town, I'm dragged along with him."

"That's cool."

"I don't think so. It's a hassle for me."

"You've got to know many people and gain friends."

"But I have to make a lot of adjustments, just like now."

"Well, that's true. That's the hardest part."

After saying it, the bell rings. Stephanie beckons me to go back to the hallway. We stride as fast as we can, and in five minutes, passing some students along the corridors, she brings me to our room. It's the first room on the second floor of the building, where a few paintings of the skeletal system hang. We're the first two to arrive. Not long enough, several students keep coming in, and our teacher, in her early fifties, I guess, comes in neat, with her paraphernalia on her hands drawn closer to her chest. She has a long neck, enough to glance at who's listening to her or not. She puts her things on the table and starts the class with an orientation. She eagle-eyes me while I'm sitting at the back next to my newfound friend.

"I believe you have a new classmate. Introduce yourself, young lady," she says in a commanding voice as she gives me... not her stern look but her authentic smile.

I hate doing this.

I stand and give a short background on myself. The girls look at me from the soles of my feet to the crown of my head, while the boys' eyes sparkle. As I'm about to sit, a group of young men comes in. The girls scream as the latecomers dash in. I can't blame them for suddenly becoming slutty because the guys are damned attractive, oozing with sex appeal. One of them looks familiar, and I try to recall where I met or saw him. He gazes at me, so I do with him, but I divert my attention quickly to our teacher. *Yum-yum, boy.*

The chairs in front of us are suddenly vacated for them.

Whoa! Are they special, or are the other boys afraid of them? I have to find out.

They take their seats while our science teacher, Mrs. Rama, shakes her head. When she puts her hands on her waist, the screams die a natural death. She lectures in biology, and the class becomes interactive. I actively participate in her discussion because science is my favorite subject. Boys fix their eyes on me, as do the head turners, but I stare back at them, giving them a wry smile. Some girls smirk, others raise their eyebrows practically to the ceiling, while a few of them beam with smiles as if telling me, "You're doing great."

After an hour, the class ends. English and history classes come next, and then, after a long hour of boring lectures, our bald teacher dismisses us for a lunch break. If I hadn't been taught good manners, I would've taken a nap. I promise you that taking history with an old, boring teacher is like listening to a lullaby— it can take anyone to heaven.

Stephanie pulls me quickly out of the room and heads to the canteen. We fall in line to get our food. I ask her if she has already paid, but she says it's free. She adds that a philanthropist donates a million pesos for our free food at school. WOW! GREAT FOR HIM, GLORY FOR US!

We find our place in front of the entrance, just enough to spy on those who are coming in. We're taking a few bites of the burger when my friend rubs my elbow with hers. I ask why, and she points her lips to our attention-seeker classmates who just came in. She's swooning when the leader of them, I presume, glares at us.

"Oh my gosh! Mr. DeVil is in the house... I mean in the canteen." Stephanie's eyes scintillate as she utters it softly. She giggles like a pig that is about to be butchered.

Devil. Did I hear it right? Steph calls him the devil. Is she crazy? Is that the look of a devil? Where's his horn and his tail? Where's his trident of eternal flame? He's not a devil; he's a demigod, you crazy eating machine.

"Why did you call him Devil?

"Because he's the DeVil."

"Seriously?" I furrow my brows, my eyes narrowing.

"Yeah. He's known here on campus as the DeVil."

"Isn't he offended?"

"Why should he?" Steph smirks. "Since childhood, that's what he's fondly called. He's used to that. Isn't it a sexy name?" She giggles again.

"Sounds awful."

"Mean."

"No, I'm not."

"Well, for your information, my dear friend, he's called DeVil because it stands for Denver Villareal."

"Oh, I see. That explains everything."

"Aha."

I keep eating, feeling like someone is eagle-eyeing me. I can sense it. I don't know why I have this strong intuition, but it all started on my fifteenth birthday. I can even feel someone spying on my dad as long as he's within my glances or with my internal GPS, as Oprah Winfrey calls it, during her Commencement Speech at Harvard University. I watch her on YouTube saying it, and that solidifies my belief that somehow she's right; after all, she's the Spiritual Queen Mother of America. Just like all moms, she knows a lot.

Speaking of gut feelings, I defended my dad at a Thanksgiving party from the punches of his green-eyed monster coworker. The man was getting near to my dad and giving him a sour look. I warned my father that he might be attacked because someone was maliciously observing him. The man's initial effort to attack my dad ended up landing on someone else's face; thus, my words came true. Poor guy. He was permanently excluded from the yearly celebration. Am I a freak?

As I'm having the last bite of my large burger, one of the guys approaches us.

"Hi, Piggy. I mean, Miss Adorable Stephanie."

"Oh, hi Therex. This is the first time you've called me Miss Adorable Stephanie. Got a high fever?"

"Nope. Let's put it this way. I realize that you're an interesting lady. I want to know you more."

"Huh? For the three years that we've been in this school, do you find me interesting now? Fool anybody, but not me, the chubby lady. Let's get straight to the point. Does DeVil command you to come here? He keeps staring at my pretty friend."

"You're unbelievable." He directs his attention to me. "Hi, I'm Therence. And you're?"

"I'm Everly."

"Nice to meet you, Everly. See you around." Therence grins widely at me. Before he glides back to his group, he has put his middle and index fingers in a V-shape, pointing to his eyes, and then directing them to Steph as if saying, 'I'm watching you.' Steph responds to him with her thumb and index finger of both hands, forming a check sign, and places them near her temples while her tongue is out.

I shake my head in disbelief. That's unladylike, but true to her words, she's a fighter. Then she pokes her face against his, mimicking his words.

"His name is Therence. Why do you call him Therex?"

"Duh," she says, rolling her eyes. "It's obvious; he looks like a dinosaur."

"He's not."

"He pisses me off by calling me Piggy, so I call him Therex because it sounds like a dinosaur. "Isn't it fair enough?"

I chuckle. She has an inner goddess of war. We resume talking until we head back to our room for the remaining classes. Our teachers lecture us with their lengthy yet informative topics, and then I hear the last bell ring. I check my watch. It's 3:15 p.m., and again, Steph pulls me out of the room and leads me to the locker to place our things. She invites me for a quick snack, but I politely decline. Dad will fetch me after class.

No wonder she gets big; eating is her favorite subject.

I stride to the parking lot and look for an old Mitsubishi car, but I can't find it. As I wait for my dad, my intuition tells me that someone's following me, and I'm right. Mr. DeVil is standing not far from where I stand, glaring in my direction. I check the place to see if there's anybody who supposedly receives his attention, but there's none. I'm right; he's smiling at me. Denver looks irresistibly hot in his signature black shirt, but not with a hood this time, and pairs it with dark jeans. *Gosh.* He ambles toward me.

I'm shaking, babe.

"Hi."

"Hi." I try to calm down, but still, my fingers are fidgeting. This is it. This is the first time a guy has ever come close to me at my age, and I don't know how to behave. I can handle difficult subjects, but not a guy. I don't know how to act in front of him.

Oh, Jesus, he's damn hot and deliciously sexy.

"I'm Denver." He reaches his hairy hand to me, but it's enough to add an extra appeal to him. It makes him more masculine. I find guys appealing when they're hairy—hairy chest, hairy hands, and legs—but not messy, and I don't know what else will be hairy. It's strange to me because most girls my age like tidy guys without mustaches or beards. Maybe he's an exception to the girls in the class because it's clear—as clear as the crystal water—that he's a cup of their tea.

"*Do they make you jealous?*" My witch horns in.

"Everly, right?"

"Yes," I quip, and suddenly feel the flames licking my fair skin as my hand shakes his. Surely, my angular face goes red. "By the way, thanks for the help last time. I know it's you."

"You're welcome. It's my pleasure to help."

"Good. Oh, my hand," I say, and he grins as he immediately releases it. I bite my lips. "Do you live near the campus?"

"It's a fifteen-minute drive from home."

"I see. Glad to hear that." I smile, and his stares bring me some sensations. I don't know why, but somehow there's some sort of connection between us. I feel I'm safe around him...with him...in him. He keeps glancing at me, biting his lips, and every time our eyes interlock, I surmise it's only him and me on this planet. It's serene; it's magical, and it seems there's a camera rolling around us. I feel I'm Juliet, and he's Romeo.

"*No, not them; their love story had a tragic ending,*" my witch retorts.

I try to think of another pair, but no one comes to mind. It sucks.

"*You're Seo Ye-Ji, and he's Kim Soo-hyun,*" my witch suggests, smiling widely.

The car honks, and I see my dad peering over the window. He gets off and nears us. Denver greets him, and they shake each other's hands. His demeanor shifts from casual to formal, as if he's trying to win dad's approval for me. *Emegesh!* (Oh, my God).

"I'm glad you know each other." Dad grins while he smiles. "At least I know someone is watching over my girl now."

Denver nods.

"If you're free, drop by anytime at our place. It's where you can see a huge Spanish house with several pine trees," Dad says, and Denver nods. "We'll go ahead." He pats Denver's shoulder, and we leave him.

I swerve around to say goodbye to him.

Denver, you're neither a thing nor a human being. You're a matchstick, and so am I. We're a perfect match made in the sky.

"Everly," Denver says my name with tenderness, like a tender, juicy hotdog, as I start walking away from him. I stop and take a side glance at him. "You take care," he adds with a broad smile.

With his smile, I'm pretty sure I'll get a perfect score on my exam in digestive and nervous systems tomorrow. Yahoo!

3

Chapter 3

I'm watching Granny while she trims her plants late in the afternoon. I want to help, but she says that her plants won't bear many flowers if somebody other than her tends to them. What? Are there plants like that?

I think they grow even with little care, as long as you water them. Granny hums while I sit on the green grasses.

Life in the countryside *is* different from the city where I used to live. I can sit on a lawn for an hour without worrying if somebody's sneaking up on me. I feel safe. I have my privacy just like now, sitting while listening to the birds as they chirp on the treetops. Molave and pine trees stand like gigantic guards, swaying their leaves to the beats of the breeze, and the different sweet-smelling flowers perfume the surroundings. There's no traffic, no pollution, the air and the water are fresh, and most of all, it's not crowded. I don't even need an air-conditioned room; it's already cold. I must admit, I have begun to love this lovely place.

My daydreaming halts when Granny speaks. "Enjoying your new home?"

"Yes, Granny," I reply. "It's serene."

Granny grins while I continue.

"I don't realize there is so much beauty in here. Granny, can I also stroll in the forest?"

"Well, if you have a companion, I will allow you to go there, but not far from the entrance."

"May I know why?"

"It's dense, and we don't know the wild animals staying there. You may cause alarm to them, and they may hurt you."

"Sounds creepy. Hmm, like what animals, Granny?"

"A snake."

"Ewww."

"A dog... a huge dog."

"I like dogs."

"You do?" Granny's eyes widen.

"Yeah. You're saying huge dogs?"

"Yes. Why?"

"Well, maybe that's a member of the pack Dad saw on the first day we'd come here."

"Your Dad saw it?" There's disbelief in Granny's voice.

I nod. "According to him, he saw it cross the street, but I didn't see it. Maybe he was right."

I could've asked Granny further about dogs, but she has shifted her attention to her plants when I become more interested in our topic. I snuggle my back on the grass. I hum as I watch the skies.The golden sun nearly kisses goodbye to the horizon. I keep humming when suddenly my heart beats fast, and I feel someone gawking at me. My intuition tells me that the living being is not far from where I am. I stand and check around, but I see no one. I rub my temple.

"Are you expecting some sort of visitor at this hour, Granny?"

"Yes, he's coming."

"You said he? So we have a male visitor?" I ask. My intuition is right. It doesn't fail me. I get a feeling he's an interesting man. Granny won't prepare snacks before we come to the lawn if she doesn't find him one.

"Granny, can I ask you something?"

"Fire away."

"How do I start this? I have this feeling that someone is coming, and I prove that I'm right. Do you have that feeling too?"

"Yes. It's a woman's intuition."

"Really?" I want to be sure if Granny has it all the time or if I'm the only one who has this skill, talent, or whatever, so I ask her further. She's the only one I can count on for this. Dad will insist it's an "effect thing" of me watching mystery shows. "Does it happen to you all the time?"

"Yes. Wait a minute, do you experience this strong intuition several times?"

I jounce my head, and her face darkens.

"We will talk later. He's coming."

I hear the sound of a fast-approaching motorbike. My heart throbs fast as it draws closer... as if tens of mice run on my chest. I don't understand why I feel this way. This is the second time it has happened. The first was when DeVil neared me in the parking lot.

Oh, my G! Is he the visitor Granny expects to come over? Why should he come here? What business does he have with her?

I see him park his vehicle under the pine tree. As he draws closer, he takes my breath away. Again, he looks impressive and hot. Only the hottest guy is named DeVil... only he deserves such a name. As usual, he's smoldering in his fit V-neck black shirt that defines his muscular upper body, and those, oh boy, sexy swimmer legs will make any woman kick another woman's ass just to sit on his lap on a trip to Jerusalem.

"Hi, Mrs. Garcia."

"Hi, Denver. I'm glad you've visited me again."

"My pleasure." Denver looks at me swiftly and directs his attention to Granny.

"Denver, my granddaughter, Everly."

"Yes, we've already met," he says in his icy voice. "Shall we go ahead, Mrs. Garcia?"

Whoa. Why a sudden change of attitude, man? Do I smell horrible enough to leave you right away and ignore my beauty? If only I had Medusa's eyes, I'd turn you into a Statue of Snub.

I raise my eyebrows to the sky as my eyes follow Mr. Snobbish.

"Sure, let's go over there." Granny points to the long bench a few meters away from me, and he does not even excuse himself. I shake my head. Granny and he walk toward the bench. They take a seat and chit-chat. Based on their expressions, the topic of their dialogue seems serious. I can see Granny's brows furrowing while Mr. Bipolar rubs his divided chin with his thumb. He's unfazed. He sits with his legs crossed over each other. He acts as if he's Mr. Grey. I spend my entire time staring at them, trying to decipher their topic. Is it about me?

"*Assuming,*" my witch mumbles.

Everly, behave... please. It can't be. I say to myself. *Why should they talk about me,* anyway? I close my eyes and heave a deep sigh to get rid of my nonsensical thoughts.

I wheel around and decide to enjoy the panoramic view of the towering pine trees. I'm not a naturalist, but seeing the wonders of creation, I can't help but be thunderstruck. My solitary moment doesn't take long when I hear someone clear his throat behind me. It's him... The Boy Who Ignores The Girl Who Likes Him.

"I don't know you have a thing for nature," Denver says.

I raise my brows and smirk at him.

"What's that for?"

"Oh, you snubbed me a few minutes ago. Now, you're asking me why I act like this view."

"Sorry."

I pout my lips.

"Look, I'm sorry."

"Fine." I give up, and I know he's smiling. "Great view here."

"Yes, whatever." I can see him roll his eyes.

The nerves. I fold my arms around my chest. "Well, I'm enjoying the view. I don't have this in a city."

"Yeah. I almost forgot you're a city girl. Do you miss the movies and concerts?"Denver asks as he puts his hands, each in his jeans' pocket.

So sexy. "Honestly, I don't. There's something in this place that makes me fall in love as the days pass by."

"Really?"

"Yes."

"So you will stay here longer?"

"I guess." I flip my long, black hair over my shoulder to clear some hairs that cover my face.

"Beautiful."

"Excuse me?"

"The view is beautiful." Denver grins, flashing his pearly white teeth.

I chortle. I overthink that he's saying it for me. I'm expecting it's meant for me, but it's the view that receives his compliment.

"Indeed." I sigh.

"What was that for?"

"What do you mean?"

"You sigh."

It's a quiet sigh. A puff of air has barely escaped my lips. *So how does he know it? His senses are strong.*

"Nothing." I lie.

"Okay. You say so. How's your first day in school."

"Just fine."

"I see. Do you like your new school?"

"I guess." Oh, God. How I wish this conversation would end soon. I can't bear the tingling sensation of electrifying my body. On the other hand, my heart says otherwise.

"Are you okay?"

"I am."

"Good. Everly," Denver pauses as if there's something he needs to tell me. The way he says my name makes my inner witch mix up a charm potion for all the depressed teens who get passed over by their crushes for free. I'm holding out for it. "I think I have to go."

I shrug, and my poor heart sobs. Denver walks a few steps away from me, but he pirouettes and says.

"It's not only the view that is beautiful, but also...you are." Denver winks at me, and my heart somersaults. It feels like I'm winning the lottery, and my witch flies with her 2024 Iron Broomstick, with its tail spewing words of congratulations.

4

Chapter 4

Rain patters on the skylight. I don't feel like going to school, but I have to.

I won't miss the chance of seeing Denver. My headache strikes again, but I still decide to go to school. I take pain relievers after eating my breakfast.

Dad drives me to school. As we head that way, I appreciate the rain more as it gently falls to the ground. It's more meaningful as it hits the trees, the plants, the flowers, and the grasses more than it does on the rooftops of shopping malls and coffee shops. I've learned from a poem written by an author whose name I've forgotten that rain, just like people, has different types. There is noisy, blustery rain that resembles talkative people; a miserable drizzle that is likened to an itinerant beggar, and a quiet rain that's similar to a gentle mother.

I kiss my dad goodbye when he parks the car at the school entrance. I clamber out, holding the umbrella. I open it and walk through the hallway. I haven't adjusted the straps of my backpack yet. I don't know why I get this feeling of laziness and detachment from my normal routine. I don't understand myself.

Really, I don't. Not too long later, I reach my room and apologize to my teacher for being late. My science teacher gives me a wry smile. I sit in my place with some vacant chairs in front of me. My forehead crinkles. My friend, the chubby girl, flashes me a smile with food residue glistening on her upper front teeth. She hands me a note, and it reads:

DeVil and his men are out when it rains.

My brow wrinkles. I don't know if my bad hair day can be attributed to his absence, but it may be the reason. I expect him to be around, but he isn't. Thoughts of him wander through my mind, trying to find the answer to why he's absent on rainy days.

Lectures from one teacher to another continue. I become disinterested in their topics, so I just stare at the window panes. The bell rings, and I hurry outside. Stephanie's mouth falls open when I come out ahead of her. I go straight to the canteen and order my food. Steph's right behind me.

I carry the tray of food and settle myself on the right wing of the canteen, near the entrance. Without saying a word, I bite the burger, and I feel that Steph's gaping at me with bulging eyes.

"Got your menstruation?" Stephanie asks.

I shake my head. "Bad hair day."

"Oh, girl's thing. Well, I have to tell you something."

Still, I continue eating and pretend I don't hear her.

"It's all about DeVil," she says, sensing if I'm interested.

Call it reflex, muscle reflex, mental alertness, or whatever, but I grab her arm and ask. "Tell me something about him."

"Oh, not so eager, huh." Stephanie teases me.

"Sorry," I say, chortling.

"Oh, there you go. You're smiling. So it's DeVil who gives you instant energy, like vitamin C."

"Stop teasing me. Common, tell me." I pinch her by her side.

"Well, during rainy days, DeVil and the boys are absent. They have this special bonding."

"What exactly is that?"

"They either play frisbee or football. And oh gosh, they are so hot because they play shirtless, and it's a joy seeing them."

"Really? They take an absence just to play?"

Stephanie brushes it off. "Well, I don't know, but I guess that's their tradition."

"Do you know their place?"

"No, not exactly. I watched it on Therex's phone."

"You do? I thought you were mortal enemies."

"Not really. During my second year here, we had this inter-rupted friendship. You know what I mean?'

"I know."

"But Therex mentions the Great Forest.

I guess that's where they play."

"Okay, thanks for the information, my friend. I think I've got to go." I stand, pulling my chair backward, and I intentionally plan to skip the afternoon classes. It's my first time doing it in my entire high school life, ever. I'll cope with it when I can. Before Stephanie could speak, I'd already dashed outside. I'll go home so I can ask Granny about the Great Forest.

Surely, she knows about it, I surmise.

I'm gliding a few meters from the canteen when my phone rings. I take it out of my pocket, and the unregistered number displays on the screen. I'm hesitant to answer it. It may be a prank caller, but my subconscious mind mutters to hit the answer button.

"Hello?"

"Everly," the voice on the other line greets me. It sounds familiar. I know it's him. Only he says my name with sexiness, but I want to be sure if it's him.

"May I know who's on the line, please?" My heart skips fast.

"It's Denver. Yeah, call me by that name."

I giggle. I can't stop myself from swooning, as if my witch has tickled my sensual bone. I bet she's grinning now with pom-poms on her hands.

"Oh, Denver, it's you." All of a sudden, I feel my energy has been restored. Stephanie's right—he's like a vitamin C for me, my energy booster. "By the way, how do you get my number?"

"From your Granny."

"I see. You're absent today. May I know why?" I want to make sure Steph's right.

"Yeah, family bonding.

"Sounds interesting!" *Ms. Piggy is right.*

"Yeah. Want to see my place?"

"I... I... I don't know." I stutter. I bite my lower lip. "I have to ask Dad."

"No worries. I believe your Granny does it for you."

I'm still doubtful about him. We barely know each other, and I can't easily give my trust to him. Maybe he senses my hesitation, so he reassures me that everything is okay.

"Don't worry. You're safe with me. Trust me. If you like, you can put me on hold while you call your Granny over."

I do what he suggests, and I call Granny. She chortles and tells me that I'm a clever girl. He further says that it's completely okay to go with him.

"Denver?"

"Yes?" His voice is sweet yet manly, as if he's teasing me to come to Daddy D.

"See you in the parking lot."

"See you in fifteen minutes."

Before his time lapses, a black Mercedes Benz has arrived, and the door on the driver's side swings open. From there, Denver comes out in his fitted sleeveless black shirt, paired again with dark jeans. *How many black jeans does he have? Doesn't he know any color other than black?*

He moves toward me, grinning, while I stand, flipping my hair back over my shoulder. His hair is wet, newly cut, and neatly combed, like Kim Soo-hyun's hairstyle.

Denver, do you know Isaac Newton? He's right about natural phenomena. I tend to be pulled by you, and so you are by me. Isn't it magical that we're brought to each other by gravity?

Denver drives while alternately looking at me. I grin back at him. We pass through some zigzag roads until we reach a huge, wide forest where towering trees abound, but there's enough space for the people to play. We get out of the car, and I see several shirtless men from afar merrily kick the ball.

The rain showers, and I click my umbrella open. Denver guides me to the bleachers and calls them. I'm feeling uncomfortable as they come close to us...so many shirtless men in here. Literally, it's raining men. If Steph were here, surely her eyes would pop out at the mouthwatering delights.

"Brothers, this is Everly. Everly, these are—

"I'm Nathaniel." The guy with a scar on his right forehead interrupts Denver and takes my hand for a handshake. He's good-looking too, with piercing gray eyes and a Greek nose on his oval face. He stands a bit shorter than Denver.

"I'm Norton," the guy chips in. He's ripped and muscular.

"I'm John Mark." He's timid.

"You know me already." Therence beams.

Each of the fifteen boys introduces himself to me.

"You must be special that DeVil brings you here. He calls you by your name. Are you his girlfriend?" Nathaniel asks. He's a bit cocky.

"I'm not. Why?"

"This is the first time he brings a lady here to our place."

I fluster scarlet. "Cool."

"I guess you'll be our lone spectator. We'll leave you for now; we need to play."

They start promenading toward the center of the meadow. Nathaniel calls Denver, beckoning him to join with them. Denver looks at me as if he's asking permission. I nod at him and tell him that it's okay to leave me for a while. He takes his shirt off and places it beside me. His muscular, hairy chest with a six-pack abdomen makes my jaw drop.

"Holy saint. Yum-yum as in yummy, right, Everly?" My witch's mouth waters, and she squelches a naughty smile.

I want to grab Denver's shirt and smell it, but I restrain myself.

The boys kick the ball and try to make a score. Denver attempts to make the first point, but Nathaniel blocks it. Sighs and laughter fill the air. As I'm watching over them, I have the feeling of urinating. My eyes wander for a portable toilet in the area, but I can't find one. I don't want to disturb Denver, so I stand and see a bush. I dart, for I can't bear the urgency to pee anymore, as if it would come out at any moment like a loose cannon. I lower my pants as I hide behind the bush. I shake my head, for I can't believe I'm peeing in the bush and not in the toilet. It's my first time. Who cares? Nobody's around—the boys are playing.

When I'm about to pull my pants up, I hear a growl, and it becomes louder as I'm done pulling my pants. I check around and freeze when I see a gray wolf flickering its tongue in and out; it's delighted to see me for its afternoon snack.

Shivers run down my spine.

I move back so I can gather all my strength and energy to run. When I do, I run as fast as I can, back to the bleacher, screaming for help. I don't turn around, for I know it's following me. In a few minutes, I glare at Denver and the boys with shock in their eyes as they see me run toward them. I see Denver's furious face, and he runs in my direction to rescue me as he shapeshifts into a black wolf before my fragile hands can touch him.

"Holy wolf. Have you seen that, honey? Your boy is a wolf." My witch widens her eyes.

"What? Wait a minute. Is this real?"I rub my eyes to check if I'm hallucinating. *What a dangerously devilish freak.*

Denver *is* a wolf! He lunges at the gray wolf, scratching its body with its claws and drawing its powerful, long legs against it. The gray wolf whines at Denver's attack. It has no match for him. Denver comes close to it, and the gray wolf turns into a young woman. Denver transforms back into himself, and I'm astounded that they have their clothes on. I surmise they'll appear before us naked, but they aren't. I'm flabbergasted. Well, it's the 21st century, and wolves do evolve.

Even if they're far away, surprisingly, I can hear their conversation.

"Stay away from us. Stay away from my girl," Denver commands at the top of his voice.

My girl? Does he just say my girl to me? Surely my inner witch is doing ten jumping jacks now.

"You violate our ancient tradition. This Great Forest is for the wolves only. How come there's a mortal here?"

"She's no ordinary mortal. Leave now before I tear you down." Denver swirls around and walks away from her, but she stands, takes a blazing knife, and dares to attack Denver.

"Stop!" I shout. She halts her attack, and I continue. "Don't stab him. You're both wolves. You don't need to hurt each other." I command as I walk toward them. "Listen to me, you'll throw that knife. Throw it, throw it now!" I fix my eyes on her. Like an obedient dog following her master, she throws the knife. "Go home in peace now." She transmogrifies into a wolf again and runs back to the woods at lightning speed.

Denver and the rest of the guys have their mouths forming an O shape in astonishment at me—maybe they're wondering how I mind-control the lady dog. If they're surprised about my ability, I'm more than petrified about myself too. I'm a *certified* freak.

Denver nighs, and my heart pounds erratically.

"Thank you for saving my life."

"You're welcome, wolf."

"Like that."

"So all of you are wolves, right?"

All of them nod.

"Does it matter to you? Are you going to stay away from me?" Denver asks me, smiling.

"No, not at all. Nothing changes."

"Thanks. So how do you do that?"

"What do you mean?"

"Oh, don't be so naïve." Denver rolls his eyes.

"I don't know. It just comes out naturally. I don't know I have this persuasion thing until I save you from the she-wolf's attack."

"And let me add, you run fast like one of us."

"I do?" My brows scrunch with confusion.

"Yes. It's one of your skills."

"What are you trying to say, I'm a wolf too, just like you?" I let out a soft laugh.

"No, you're far greater than us," he says in a serious tone. "When the right time comes, your Granny and I will explain everything to you. But for now, let's take a rest and perhaps grab some snacks."

Denver offers his hand to me, and I take it. Warm currents electrify my body, and it feels good, baby.

We head to a small house situated not far from the bleacher. An old man welcomes us into his abode and offers something to eat. Denver thanks him, and he smiles at him. The boys rush to grab some, and I take the cookies.

Denver mouths, "Let's get outside."

I nod, and we walk outside. We find ourselves sitting on the long wooden bench. His presence gives me serenity, but something in my mind tells me that there's imminent danger with him. I choose to listen to my heart.

"Everly," he says with his penetrating gaze, crash-landing on me.

"Yes," I reply in my girlish tone, but I'm sure my witch is wetting.

"Promise me that you'll stay as a nice girl."

"Of course."

"Promise me that you'll never leave your house alone."

"I will, master."

"Everly," he says it, not with a question mark but rather a statement.

"Yes?"

"Will you be my girl?"

I choke, and Denver rubs my back.

Ah, gentleman.

"Does silence mean yes?" He playfully raises his eyebrows.

"You have to court me."

"Is there a need for that? I can sense that you—

"Wolf." I cut him off. I know he senses that I like him too. "You need to."

"Just kidding," Denver grins and offers three red roses to me. "So let the courtship begin."

I chortle. I sniff the flowers while looking at him. "Thanks."

"Anytime for my girl."

I bite my lips, and he winks at me. I'm sure his Calvin Klein briefs drop on his ankles.

"Den, you know what? You steal my heart."

Denver moves toward me and whispers. "And I return it with interest."

My heart ricochets, and my Bench's panties lower.

I can feel my inner witch light the entire woods with ten thousand torches, and then she flies skyward and dives from the sky, not with her broom but with her pink parachute.

5

Love Poems

Why Do I Love You?

Why do l love you?
I love you because I love being you;
Bold.
Brainy.
Beastly.
Why do I love you?
I love you because you love me being me;
Stubborn.
Stupid.
Sweet.
Why do I love you?
I love you because you complete me.
I love you because you make me happy.
I love you because you never fail
to court me every single day.
I love you because I love only you.

***

Wonders Of Love

Love has no eyes, but it makes me see you,
even in darkness. It doesn't have feet,
but it always leads me back to you
amidst stormy days.
It doesn't have ears, but you listen to me
even if you have doubts.
It doesn't have the power of speech
because that's how it is.
Love doesn't always need to be voiced out.
It isn't a word meant to be spoken.
It's a feeling that deaf can hear,
a blind can see,
a mute can grumble,
and a fool may understand.
These are the wonders of love.

***

Colors Of Love

When I'm in love
I see colors everywhere,
oceans are aquamarine,
mountains are forest green,
your shirt is mint;
Butterflies are hue,
skies are blue,

so your eyes too;
Roses are red,
ants are vermilion
your cheeks, persimmon;
Raven is black,
so are bats,
your midnight hair waltzed;
Yellow is the sun
yellow-red is the sunset
But your heart is gold, not scarlet.

***

Only Fools Believe In Love

Only fools believe in love
Only fools believe in forever,
Only fools believe in you.
Let me be a fool then.

Poetry is for the fools
Poetry is the language
of the soul,
Methink, I'm foolish.
Let me be a forever fool then.

***

Wings Of Love

I'm an angel, you're the devil,

yet we love each other.
You fight for me,
I disobey my Master,
so we're outcast from our peers.
Let's fly to Wonderland
or fathom the deepest ocean
and consume our affection.
Heaven has no place for the devil
nor hell for an angel,
Lovers we are;
Lovers we die.
And a lightning bolt ends our lives.

6

The Halfling

"The biggest adventure you can ever take is to live the life of your dreams."
-Oprah Winfrey

"An nadamu tu ina igisum amargi. I bequeath you the gift of immortality," the omniscient Horn of Flames, surrounded by a swirling vortex of fire, muttered in a loud-booming voice. The holy ground of Mount Zhegai shook as he spoke. Black—and—gray clouds slathered, thunder rumbling and flashes of lightning tearing the sky.

Being the creator of the Ebabbar and the Badgaldinger, the omnipotent Horn of Flames spoke of tongues no living beings could understand except the Tammabukkua, the Dimunes, and the Saint Mermaid.

The scorching Horn of Flames summoned the Tammabukkua or the dragons to bow down before him. The dragons lowered their heads, wings locked and tails fiddled.

"We will rule the Badgaldinger, the Lu Matum, and the

Kharsaanu Saquutu together. The mermaids, the merfairies shall become our food, and the mortals, our slaves. Maharu annu igisum neperdu."

Out from the Horn of Flames, the fiery lightning rods came out and floated toward the dragon king and the dragon queen. The rods perched on their heads and turned into crowns flashing with bolts of lightning. And lo, the dragons had shape-shifted into human-like forms.

The king and queen donned cerise cloaks, showcasing their exquisite beauty that surpassed the movie stars or even the angels in heaven. Their fair-skinned hands shimmered like diamonds, and their thick raven hair waltzed with the wind. Their auras were regal, and their smiles devilishly alluring—enough to enchant an innocent soul into a painful death.

"Nam-še Utuk Xul Dingir Xul." The queen curtsied with gratitude. "Nam-še."

With high spirits, the king and the queen slashed their palms and offered the cardinal blood that dripped from them to the altar of the Horn of Flames—the Great One.

The eternal vortex of fire surrounding the Horn of Flames rained down and consumed the blood.

The king and queen swirled their bodies in a snake dance led by the star dancer, the Bakunawa, an astronomical winged snake, to the beats of a hundred owls' hoots.

Balls of fire that appeared and hung like colossal chandeliers in the sky lit up the night. Flammagenitus shrouded them, but vanished in misty smoke when the Bakunawa blew acidic liquids.

"Dimunes," the Horn of Flames thundered. The yucky creatures shivered in fear. "Gather yourselves before the king and queen. Bow to no one but to the king, queen, and me."

The Dimunes with disfigured faces, bloodshot eyes the size of golf balls, and who stood three-feet inches tall, knelt and bowed down before the Horn of Flames, the king, and the queen.

They kept bowing and singing a hymn of praises.

Santi, Santa, and Santo chanted. "Holy, holy is the Great One. Holy is thy name. Worthy to receive honor and praise and power."

A hundred Dimunes said, "Amen." They taunted, "Worthy are the lambs that were slain, for they'd receive nothing but disgrace, mockery, and misery.

Afterward, the Dimunes slaughtered, roasted, and bolted down the nine hundred and ninety-nine lambs. The Dimunes' immortal friends—the ravens—they crammed down the grilled lambs' eyes in the sangria sticks.

Two powerful ravens feasted on sixty-six percent of the eyes while three of the greatest Dimunes devoured thirty-four percent of the meat."

"Savory," Rowling-the-raven croaked. "I want more."

"Succulent, damn it." King-the-raven cursed, his saliva driveled. Rowling and he even played Roshambo, a rock-paper-scissors game, using each right foot to get the last pair of the corpse's eyes. Rowling won.

"Yummy, curse, curse, curse it," Santi screeched. His three horns on his head pointed skyward, and his six wings made him a Seraphzim, the leader among the Dimunes. He was also the supreme right hand of the Horn of Flames, having the strength of a hundred vultures. He bit the glowing purple skin of his brother Dimunes like a vampire and sucked their blood like a leech.

"Toothsome, curse, curse, curse it," Santo squeaked. He nudged the shoulders of the other Dimunes. He had three horns on his head and four wings—two on his back and two on his feet, and the Dimunes called him a Quartzim.

"Luscious, curse, curse, curse it," Santa squawked. Just like Santo, he was a Quartzim too. Among the three, Santa was the most magnanimous and the smartest. He shared whatever meat he'd got with his brothers.

While the king and queen ate modestly from a long black glass table, a hundred Dimunes gobbled up the roasted meat like hungry beasts. In a few seconds, the lambs were nothing but bones. Alternately, they slurped the lambs' fresh blood from a vermilion goblet. The Dimunes' mouths watered as they licked the bones, squawking merrily as they swore at the heavenly food.

All night long, the Dimunes, the king and queen danced, sang and leaped with merry hearts in gratefulness for the immortality the Horn of Flames had bestowed them.

"How do we call the mortals?" the dragon queen asked.

"Dust-blood," the Dimunes chorused.

"How about the mermaids and the merfairies?" the dragon king asked.

The Dimunes thought hard.

Santa wrote his answer on the air with the letters on fire.

WARTHOG

"Imbecile," Santi shouted. "It doesn't ring a bell. No brilliance, no magic."

Santa rearranged the letters.

HOGWART

"Nincompoop," Santi yelled. "A billionaire merfairy-author, K. J. MacSpellbound, already copyrights it. K. J. will sue us for copyright infringement under the International Statute of Copyrighted Titles and Materials of the Magical Beings if we use that.

"Besides, I've heard she's a 'KJ'," he adds with air quotes in the last two letters of his statement. "KJ which stands for Kill Joy. The initials work out for her."

"Feeling all-knowing," Santo whispered. "I know Santa's idea will be handpicked."

"Shut up!" the dragon queen roared. "Warthog then."

Santo winked at Santa.

The Horn of Flames let out a boisterous laugh.

Before the dawn struck, a spectacle of fireworks with green, red, and purple lights shaped in the images of dragons, unicorns, goats, flowers, fish, fairies, mermaids, and merfairies had the Dimunes' jaws dropped.

Even the Saint Mermaid couldn't contain her astonishment— her one eye seemed to pop out.

Then the Horn of Flames... the Dark Lord Dingir Xul Vander-worse growled with menace.

"Being the distinguished guest of the sacred bestowal, I forbid you, Naruha, from revealing the secret, or else I *will* curse you. For whoever could defeat the dragons would possess the crowns to be wielded as the most powerful weapon ever known to exhume the dark forces.

"If this happens, the dragons will obliterate from the face of the Badgaldinger. I don't want that to happen. Níg-ge-gid-da bel ade u mamit?"

"I understand, Dark Lord." Naruha nodded, plucked a few scales on her tail, and blew it to the Horn of Flames as a symbol to keep her promise. The Horn of Flames laughed mischievously and scorched the covenant of scales. The Saint Mermaid's brows flinched.

And the Dark Lord spoke of an unspeakable horror.

"Naruha summa tu parasu zi-gi-es-en ana qamu tu nig ina

a-a-še mu-un-da isatum."

"I will never dare, Dark Lord." Naruha bowed with humility and loyalty to serve the Horn of Flames for all eternity. "Now, if you excuse me."

Feeling dreadful of the events, Naruha navigated on a floating body of waters back to her dominion.

Under the dark sea-bottomed cave at Mermailandia, Saint Mermaid Naruha had sprawled on a shimmering-huge-scalloped shell.

She spun her vermilion tail, fashioning a roller coaster of purple whirlpools for her schools of anchovies. She clapped, and hundreds of diminutive scallops drifted on the eddies.

She snapped her fingers, and six hundred and sixty-nine dinoflagellates deflagrated overhead.

The cave walls suddenly glistened with gold, pearls, and precious stones, and the pearly white sand lay on the floor, visible in the crystal clear, blue waters.

The anchovies' eyes effervesced, and they swam to navigate on the scallops; and they arranged themselves by ten. They screamed in merriment as the whirlpools moved. They glided and tumbled, yelling and shouting with stars in their eyes.

Naruha hummed while watching the high-spirited anchovies.

Mounted on the cave's wall right behind Naruha, the Naru Clock, made of Capiz and Sigay shells, seaweeds, and seahorses that served as the long and short hands, screeched at midnight.

The Anchovies Alertness and Motivation Game ended.

Naruha puffed some air, and the Naru Clock vanished from sight. She whistled, and the anchovies on their scallops came near her. She cleared her throat, and the anchovies gazed at her, patiently waiting to listen to her most fantastic lecture. She winked, and the whirlpools made their way out to the cave's well until they slowly dissipated. She swished her trident, and the letters formed in water hung in the air read *The Cosmogony and the Dark Lord's Master Plan.*

The anchovies widened their eyes with amazement. Naruha flipped her sanguine hair, grinning at them. "Let's test your knowledge, my dear allies."

"Aye," the anchovies said in unison.

Naruha cleared her throat. "Badgaldinger?"

"Wonderworld," a tiny anchovy answered.

"Very good! And Utuk Xul?"

"Evil Spirit," a tinier anchovy replied.

"Awesome."

"I am," the tinier interjected. The anchovies cackled at her air of arrogance.

"Ebabbar?"

"House of the Rising Sun or Underfireworld," the tiniest anchovy screeched.

"Impressive." Naruha winked at her. The tiniest anchovy grinned at Naruha's compliment. The tiny and the tinier anchovies caressed their tiniest sister's fin. "Small but smart."

"She is," a tinier anchovy chimed in again. The schools of anchovies chuckled.

"Hmmm. Tammabukkua?"

The cave fell silent. The anchovies' eyes flinched with horror. For a few minutes, Naruha waited for their answers, but no one dared. Smiling, Naruha knew her anchovies were frightened to mention the creature. Until the oldest anchovy coughed and swam to near her.

"Dragons."

"Very brave, Oldest One. Like your oldest brother, you must all be courageous, for time will come that you'll face your greatest enemy. Without courage, you can never defeat the evil. Without fortitude, you can't have hope. Without hope, life is meaningless." Naruha cocked her head. The anchovies were gobsmacked at her brilliance. "For your knowledge, the Dark Lord had turned the *dragons* into human-like forms."

"Unbelievable." The Oldest quipped. "Terrible idea."

"Why do you say so?"

"They can now easily mingle among us and turn us into their subjects."

"At their mercy?" Naruha shook her head. "Never will it happen for so lon' as you're under my protection."

"How about the Dimunes, yes, the Dimunes," the tiniest of the anchovies interrupted. "Are they for real?"

Naruha's lips twitched. "They are."

"How do they look like?"

"If I may be honest, I would find the Tasmanian Devil more gorgeous than them."

"Yuck," the tiniest anchovy rolled her eyes. "That means, they're very ugly." And all the anchovies had belly laughs. "Scary as well?"

"They are."

"Oh, I see," the anchovy with a large snout said. "S–S–So— the rumor is true—they're real and scary. Now I'm scared."

"You must be. Their favorite meal is the tiny creatures like... you." Naruha joked. "The Dimunes were born with the matin' of the Horn of Flames and a virgin sea-nymph, Nina Idimmu. So that explains why they're terrifyin' and powerful."

"Oh, I'm dead." And he acted as if he were dead as his brothers yelled 'play dead' at him.

"And they eat lambs like the voracious sharks."

"Whoa!" the anchovies echoed. "The Dimunes are certified

beasts, Saint Mermaid," said one of them with the second to the largest snout.

"And the Dark Lord Dingir Xul Vanderworse said... "

"What did the Dark Lord say?" the anchovy with the most oversized snout asked while its dear brother and sister anchovies' snouts trembled with horror upon hearing the Dark Lord's name. "Please, Great Naruha, don't mention his name anymore; it makes my fins quiver."

"I will." Naruha's eyelashes twirled. "The Dark Lord will burn me alive in the lake of fire should I dare to disobey him."

"An accomplished evil!" the tiniest anchovy commented on Naruha's revelation, its snout quavering.

Naruha grinned at the tiniest and caressed its head. "He is. I'd shuddered at the thought of gettin' barbecued alive, but my visions told me only a half-Dustler, half-merfairy could defeat the dragons. Only he could summon the powers of the lightnin' spear. Only he," Naruha mumbled.

"A half-Dustler?" asked the youngest anchovy. "W-What does it mean?"

"A half-mortal. A two-legged human bein' who looks like the one livin' in the coastal areas, and the one who catches fish," Naruha explained while smiling at the innocence of the youngest. Little did he know a Dustler caught anchovies for his food.

"Is he the same as the ones who catch big fish?" the youngest furthered. Naruha nodded. "Oh, I see." The youngest anchovy flipped his dorsal fins. "How about a half-merfairy?"

"He has a man's body, a fairy's wing, and the huge fish's tail."

"Perfect. He must be powerful then."

"I surmise. He'll come to fulfill his destiny."

"The Mesha?" asked the tinier anchovy, eyes glistering. "I mean, the One, the savior?"

"Yes."

"Is he a highly sophisticated, intellectually gifted species like you?"

"I think he's smart."

"Is he warm and kind?"

"I believe so."

"Great. But is he coming?"

"Certainly, certainly. He's comin', my dear," Naruha answered, her pearl covering her left eye glittering. Her hair hanging down her ankles glistened, and her sunken face glimmered enough to light up the entire kingdom. "The Halflin'. He's comin' very soon."

The sun rose and set for a thousand years, but Naruha never lost her hope that the Redeemer would come someday.

Until one magical night, Naruha glared at the moonless sky, and seventeen meteorites showered endlessly.

"Finally, the time has come."

Several kingdoms and a thousand miles away, an adolescent boy prophesied to save the magical worlds, had washed his car, and his piercing aquamarine eyes smoldered with excitement for a journey of a lifetime.

"Mom, I saw it with my naked eyes," a sixteen-year-old boy began, his eyes the shade of the ocean burning with excitement and revelation. His mom raised his eyebrows practically to the ceiling of the dining room upon hearing his words. "Granny froze an owl. Isn't that amazing?" he told his mom at breakfast about the strange things he'd witnessed about his grandmother during his last visit.

Since he'd been eleven years old, he had long suspected his

Granny had magical powers—at the very least, a witch who could transfigure into a crow, a canine, or a cat. He'd caught her talking to a blue butterfly, freezing owl mid-air, and bringing dead black mice back to life. She was *not* human.

But his mom always discredited him.

"You're over-imagining, son," Mrs. Ashtor said in her honey voice, slicing the roasted turkey with her Monarch Steampunk Dragon Knife, very designer. She was curvaceous and blonde. "Ferro, my dear, your Granny can't even lift her finger to a mouse, much less an owl. That's what you get when you play too many Mobile Legends." Her azure eyes flickered with a warm gaze as she sat across from him. "Hot chocolate?"

And his beefy dad, whose round eyes sparkled a thousand dollars every time a resort guest came in, would scare him off while sipping his tea in a chicken cup from the Qing Dynasty. "Ferro Ashtor, girls don't like boys who make up stories. And worse, weird guys. A major turnoff for them."

Uh-oh. Coming from a certified chick boy. "I think so, Dad." Ferro nodded in agreement, grinning. Even if it was the end of the world, neither he wanted girls to call him weird nor his image of being a chick magnet to be stained. Not in the private school where girls giggled—their ovaries practically exploded—when he passed them in the corridors. Not on his seventeenth birthday. Not in a company of charm and chicks where he'd been the chief executive officer.

"Just like Bill," his mom whispered in between her bites.

"Maybe, like Uncle Bill, I have a wild imagination," he added, trying to brush off the magical-granny idea. Even though he knew from the inner core of his heart, his granny was no ordinary woman. His mom and dad both shrugged. "I need to go." Ferro stood, slightly smacking the table with his hands, nearing his mom and kissing her goodbye. For his dad, he gave him a quick, playful salute.

"Aren't you staying for your coming birthday?" his mom asked. Ferro shook his head.

"Like father, like son," his dad commented. Ferro let out a loud laugh while his mom gave his dad a stern look.

Ferro drove his Mercedes Benz to Aloguinsan, a mountain town of Cebu and home of his Granny, whom he'd imagined on an occasion or two as a white witch whose chin could slice a black forest cake.

He was wearing his favorite Georgio Armani white tee-shirt, black jeans, and white sneakers, and this signature style had made him the cover boy of his school magazine issue in 2016.

Very Shawn Mendesish.

Simply sweltering and charming.

He rolled the window halfway down as he passed the highway. The summer solstice air smooched his light brown skin, reminding him of his Granny's warmth and wisdom, and the Instagrammable landscapes, shrubs, and trees under the clear, blue skies wowed his eyes. He even took his Bentley Platinum sunglasses off for a minute or two to fully appreciate their splendor.

He sped up the car—tires screeching—to finally reach the haven of Bojo River, excited to meet his Granny, who preferred to be with her butterflies and birds than live a day or two in their Mactan, Lapu-Lapu resort spa.

Ferro cocked his head on his right side, and a set of pearly white teeth flashed from a lady who liked him more than a friend. She was Lyzabeth, his Saturday girl.

Sensing the deafening silence behind him, he viewed the Mobile Legend hero wannabes in a side mirror... introducing his friends of foolishness, Brad and Nathaniel.

Ferro drummed his fingers on the wheel as he wound the highway. He turned on the music, held Lyzabeth's hand, and smacked it. The Witch in the Academy of Flirts moved closer to him and planted a long, sweet kiss on him. Meanwhile, the two hobgoblins in the back seat were busy playing the Bang Bang.

Ferro blasted the music to the tune of Despacito, and the hobgoblins became the living souls. They sang and shimmied while holding their phones. Even Lyzabeth couldn't control her inner Salome and joined their playfulness.

Suddenly, an image of a winged lady came into Ferro's mind.

"Hey Brad, want to drive my best buddy?" Ferro asked as he lowered his sunglasses.

"Hell, yeah. It's my dream to ride this limited edition car of yours," Brad replied, eyes exhilarated, and his smiles nearly reached his rat-like ears. He was thin and dark-skinned.

Ferro parked the car on the roadside while Brad clambered out from the back seat.

While his friends were chanting and dancing, Ferro took a nap. Often when he closed his eyes, he dreamed he was slashing a flaming-gigantic female creature with a blazing spear and scuffled to fight against the dragons and the dark forces of the wicked witch.

Good boy didn't tell his mom and dad about it; his inner god hissed. *Did you, chick boy?*

However, his nightmares turned into a beautiful vision when a woman of striking beauty with golden wings and a black tail materialized before him—chortling, nearing, and giving him a tender kiss.

Every time he got carried away with her, she evanesced, leaving him speechless with sparkling specks of dust on his face.

Naughty girl. I'll bite your lip if I get a chance. Ferro scowled.

Ferro awoke with a giddy smile while his friends chuckled at his inspired expression.

The sun nearly kissed goodbye to the horizon when they arrived. The gentle breeze, the hooting of the owls, and the twittering of the ravens welcomed them.

Ferro instructed Brad to pull the car to a stop near the Victorian-inspired house. The woman in her early sixties stood outside it and waved her hand at a group of teenagers who'd just gotten out of the car.

"Granny Delphina, I'm here!" Ferro said while running, whose grins flashed upon seeing the older woman.

"Ferro Ashtor, is that you, dear honey dear?" asked Mrs. Ora Delphina. Ferro jounced his head. "You've grown into a fine, young, handsome man. I barely recognize you, if not for your dimples. I miss you so much, my grandson." Her Persian blue eyes glinted in the thick, square spectacles, her plaid blouse and skirt couldn't overshadow her commanding presence, and her blonde hair in a tight bun—always styled this way then and now—held the saying true that the woman's hair is her crowning glory.

"I miss you too, Granny. You don't age. You still look in your early forties." Ferro hugged her, but he couldn't wrap his arms around her waist. Yes, his Granny was right. He'd aquamarine eyes with an aquiline nose sculpted in an oval face that stunned the city girls, and his lean yet muscular build made them bite their lips. Girls would've mistaken him for Shawn Mendes's doppelgänger.

"Oh, thank you very much, dear," and she whispered to herself, *If only Ferro knew how old I was, he'd be more gobsmacked.*

"That's why I love you so much."

Ferro bussed his Granny's right cheek and introduced his friends Lyzabeth, Nathaniel, and Brad to her.

Ferro and his friends sauntered inside and sat bolt-upright on the wooden chairs. They cheerfully gourmandized the lasagna, bacon strips, and clubhouse sandwiches. Their stomachs lurched for more, and their thirsts quenched when they slurped a glass of algid Ora Chocolatte.

"Granny, your Ora Chocolatte is the yummiest chocolate drink I've ever tasted," Ferro muttered. "No drinks in the province of Cebu could equal its taste. Someday, every child in the world will drink your Chocolatte."

"You think so?" Mrs. Delphina's eyes effervesced. "I hope so, my dear honey dear. I make my Ora Chocolatte using native cacao, stirring it with sugar, syrupy smiles, and love. Thank you very much."

"You're very much welcome. By the way, Granny, is the bridge still passable?" Ferro asked, his fingers tapping on the wooden table which could accommodate the Twelve Apostles of the Last Supper.

"Shh, don't mention it, dear honey dear," hushed Mrs. Delphina. "It's nearly evening. The she-creature might hear you.

"How did you know it's she, not he?" *Creepy Granny.*

"I just know it," answered Mrs. Delphina while rolling her eyes.

"Why do you keep calling she-creature? Doesn't she have a name until now?"

Shaking her head, Mrs. Delphina stared at her grandson. *If there were something that didn't change about Ferro since he'd been a little boy, they were his inquisitiveness and appreciativeness;* she thought. She didn't say a word; instead, she responded to him with a wry grin. She was about to rise when a great splash from the river a few meters away from her house resounded.

A brilliant lightning flash unexpectedly brightened the dining room, and thunder raged and rattled the windowpanes. The rain fell hard with horrifying screams.

Ferro heard them, his forehead scrunched with shock, and his friends' upper eyelids cowered.

Another one followed by a splash.

The lights went out.

Lyzabeth held Brad's left forearm while Brad clung to Nathaniel's right arm—shivers ran down their spines.

However, Ferro remained unfazed.

The chickens in Mrs. Delphina's backyard cackled. Ferro stretched his arms as he yawned. His friends wiped their eyes with bare hands.

"Boys, come on down, breakfast time," said Mrs. Delphina as she prepared the food while the slender, round face and shouldered-length-hair-brunette Lyzabeth assisted her.

After swishing their mouths with Dr. Harold Katz's chlorine dioxide and washing their faces in the lavatory, Ferro and the boys ambled to the wooden dining table.

"Did you remember anything last night, boys?" Lyzabeth asked briskly.

The boys shook their heads.

"Why, what happened, Lyza?" Ferro asked.

"Oh, nothing significant, Fer," Lyzabeth replied, staring at Mrs. Delphina and mouthing, "The incantation worked."

Mrs. Delphina simpered sheepishly, still wondering why her spell didn't affect Lyzabeth. Only the boys were. There must be something special about this lady.

"Granny, can we go to the bridge later?" Ferro asked with excitement in his voice.

"No." Mrs. Delphina shook her head, her index finger raised right above her shoulder, emphasizing her disapproval. "Big no, dear honey dear."

"Please, Granny, please!" Ferro pleaded with puppy eyes. The boys stood, surrounding the older woman, and didn't stop begging until she gave in to their pleas.

"All right, you win." Mrs. Delphina sighed. "You can go there, but promise me one thing, dear."

"Anything Granny," the boys chorused.

"Just say it, Granny, and we will do it," Ferro assured her.

"Promise me that when you cross the bridge, you'll have a sign of the cross or you'll never cross the bridge for the rest of your life."

The boys bobbed their heads, but their adventurous eyes and smiles couldn't wait to see the mysterious bridge. As soon as they emptied their plates, they hurried outside the house, nudged each other's shoulders, and scuttled to the bridge.

They forgot to kiss Mrs. Delphina on her cheeks. Lyzabeth decided to stay with the woman.

Only Ferro did a sign of the cross when they reached the old, rugged bridge.

The serenity of the river, which sparkled like crystals in broad daylight, calmed their restless spirits. The zephyr that billed their faces scented like a baby's breath and the sunshine, mother's ardor.

They stopped at the center.

"Holy wow! Truly beautiful," Nathaniel said, his slanted eyes shimmering. He was towering and got a buff body that made girls think he was the last descendant of Goliath. "Perfect for my proposal!"

Ferro and Brad chortled while listening to him.

"I doubt. Your girlfriend doesn't like romantic stuff like this, giant," Brad said. "Right, Ferro?"

"I agree," Ferro replied. "Angelina doesn't have a thing for nature."

"Okay, you win, guys, but for now, let's have a groupie," Nathaniel suggested. They'd pictured themselves facing their backs on the river.

They wandered with cheerful hearts to the other side of the bridge, going to the sturdy oak trees where they'd lean and take some more pictures.

"Guys, I have a story to tell you," Brad said, as he squatted under the tree. "This is the greatest story man had not ever known."

"Make sure it's funny." Ferro mused as he remained standing with folded arms on his chest.

"Or I will trap you here, dwarf," Nathaniel chortled, taking a seat across from him.

"Well, I don't know how you would react, guys, but I bet it is."

"Go ahead," Ferro said.

"The story is all about the three sperm cells. Once upon—" Brad started.

"Interesting!" Ferro chimed in. "Fire away."

"Once upon a time, there were three sperm cells who considered themselves not only friends but also brothers." Brad continued in a husky voice. "Let's name them John, Jay, and Judas. They dreamed of being the greatest in the distant future, except for Judas. John said," I'll be the greatest architect of all time. I'll build magnificent buildings and houses that can withstand the strongest earthquake man has ever known, and the strongest tornadoes can never destroy them. "

"Holy cow," Ferro and Nathaniel said in unison.

"I, the mighty Jay, will be the greatest scientist who can discover the universal pill curing any global diseases caused by viruses and bacteria. I'll name this pill as UniJayPil." Brad furthered in a sober tone and changed his voice into a husky.

Nathaniel nodded while Ferro said, "Amazing."

Brad went on. "John and Jay gave each other a high five for their lofty dreams. Then, John asked. "How about you, Judas? What's your dream?" Judas wiggled his tail while staring at his friends, but before he could answer, Jay said, "Make sure it's for the best of humanity. Not just for yourself." Judas shouted, "Foolish!" John's and Jay's tails pitted-a-patted with surprise at Judas's remarks. "How could you be the greatest when you and I are in the throat of a gay man?"

Ferro and Nathaniel gasped and got lost on Earth for a millisecond. When they regained their senses, Ferro and Nathaniel laughed their hearts out loud.

"That's the fate of the three Best Sperm Cells," Brad concluded with a curt bow.

"Brilliant!" Ferro clapped.

"Nice one, brother." Nathaniel lauded.

And they rolled on the ground laughing.

"Seriously, I have high respect for gay men, guys," Ferro said. "My Uncle Bill is one of them, and he's a dignified man."

"I agree." Brad smiled. Nathaniel gave Ferro a high five.

While the boys vegged under a tree, Ferro couldn't get his mind off the beauty of the river. His curious eyes made him gawk at the bridge. He left gingerly when his friends carved their names on a tree.

Ferro heard someone sing when he was nearing the bridge.

"What a sweet voice." Ferro complimented her and took his shirt off to get a nice tan.

The voice became louder as Ferro positioned at the center.

A gentle swash piqued his interest, making his brows crease. A figure of a woman with a round face, deep-seated-emerald-green eyes, and long, black hair loomed in the water.

Slutty fox. She's yummy.

The woman drew close to him. Ferro dropped his mouth open as he saw no legs on the woman but a tail. His scary bone quailed a bit.

"Fear not Ferro, for I am a friend," the woman in her sexy voice said, her eyes enigmatic.

"How did you know my name?" Ferro's eyebrow furrowed. The woman didn't answer him, but kept gaping at his body. Her mouth formed an O-shape. He couldn't blame the water girl, for, in a Parliament of Sexiness, he was the Prime Minister.

"I repeat, how did you know my name?" *Freak.*

"Oh, you've forgotten me. Perhaps your Granny did some incantations. That meshuga!" She flipped her tail, creating bubbles and ripples on the surface while the two Great Horned owls named Kim-and-Chloe-the-Owldashians fluttered around her. They rolled their eyes at Ferro.

Oh. Dangerously delicious and deliciously dangerous.

"What do you mean?" Ferro's lips curled in confusion. He sensed danger in her voice. He readied his inner god for a few karate moves.

"I'm your childhood friend. I'm Olivia, an enchantress of this river. We used to swim in this river when we were still kids."

"What? I'm sorry, miss, but I didn't remember you. I need to go." *You're a freak.*

"You can't go," Olivia spoke with authority. "Not. Now."

"Excuse me?" Ferro raised his voice. He shivered at the venom in her statement. *Demanding freak.*

"I said you can't go." Olivia gnarled and pitched her tail. She conjured a vortex while Ferro remained motionless, seeing the water move at the she-creature's wish. A gigantic snake emerged from a black whirlpool and assailed him—its body besieged his. It lifted him in the air while she hee-hawed to an old friend who suffered from being uncooperative.

Nonplussed about what Olivia did to him, Ferro snarled at her. "Let me go, or my Granny will deal with you!" *Freak fish!*

"In your dreams."

"Release him!" growled a woman's voice from a distance, her eyes ablaze with rage at Olivia but with concern for Ferro. "Or else—"

"Or else what? Turn my tail just like yours?" Olivia asked, cachinnating.

The voice came nearer, and Ferro caught another she-creature like Olivia, but her tail was different. It was black, black as a blood diamond.

Heavenly delight. She's yummier than the formidable freak.

The black-tailed she-creature fashioned a whirlpool by flinging her tail, and a gargantuan eagle sprang up and flew in Ferro's direction. It nuked the giant snake with its talons, but the snake fought harder.

Ferro panted, for he couldn't believe his eyes it happened before him. It seemed he was watching a few fighting scenes in a movie. He screamed for help while falling from the sky because the snake slackened its grip on him.

An eagle glided fast, catching and bringing him to a safer place. The eagle wheeled back, and the snake smote it with its tail. The eagle groaned. They charged at each other until the snake fell into the waters.

"Enough of this!" blustered the black-tailed woman.

"Okay then," Olivia smirked, her tone agreeable. "I wish I could win a Golden Globe Lifetime Achievement Award for following you."

"Stay away from him," she ordered.

"I will, but these guys coming, they're none of your business." Olivia lobbed her tail and formed a whirlpool. It bobbed up the octopus's tentacles and ensnared Nathaniel and Brad, Pitt eyes balled out in surprise. They bayed for help, but the black-tailed woman glared at them. The boys struggled for their lives, but their efforts seemed in vain, for an octopus's beak pierced, ripped, and broke them into smithereens. The acetabulum and the infundibulum of an octopus squelched with delights for the incomparable nutrients they'd get from the torn bodies.

Ferro watched his friends die mercilessly. He gawked at the black-tailed woman with misted eyes, but she turned her face away, submerged her body into the water, and she and the eagle dematerialized with a spin of her tail.

He gave Olivia a wine-that-could-turn-into-blood look while Olivia smiled at him in a sneeringly withering way before she disappeared into the waters.

Ferro fell to his knees and wailed.

What explanation must I have for their parents? That freak creature smashed their sons? I'd have a hard time explaining it. It would only mean two things. Either way, I was crazy or an accomplice to the crime.

He wiped his tears with his white shirt's right sleeve.

The shameless Olivia's laughter reverberated throughout the river while Ferro's heart sang an ode of lamentation.

Still facing the river, Ferro stood with feigned fortitude. *You must pay for this, freak.*

Plunk. Plunk. Plunk. Rain poured down with madness against Ferro's head, and thunder roared like a jungle king. The ravens shrieked, and the owls tu-whit tu-whoo as they flitted and perched on the branches of an oak tree.

Ferro smacked his palm against his forehead in disbelief that his friends were gone in the river. The idea of losing them didn't sink in on him yet. Their value for him was priceless, above rubies and diamonds.

"I'll avenge your death, brothers. I promise that." His nostrils smoked with anger. He punched the tree trunk and subconsciously cracked it with one strike.

His heart sank, and his feet didn't lead him home. The bright glare of lightning lightened his way, and a swirling ball of blue flames blossomed before him.

"Ferro, don't let your hatred blind you," a sweet voice from the swirling ball spoke.

"And who are you?" Ferro asked in a sarcastic tone, unsurprised by another unearthly phenomenon.

"It doesn't matter who I am."

"It matters to me. I must know my enemy before I die. Do you want to kill me? Make my day." His internal GPS of senses gave way, and he groomed for whatever destiny had been in store for him.

The voice sighed. "Call me Manara. I understand you're upset and deeply hurt, but never allow these feelings to make you forget who you are."

"Thanks for the advice. May I know why you came to speak to

me?"

"I come to tell you that no matter where you go or how dark your life is, don't forget who you are. Even in the darkest times, there's always light. There's someone waiting for you back home—to give you hope. Always remember that."

"Sounds like my Granny. Thanks."

"Walk straight, and you'll find a house. Someday, we'll meet, and I'll be the one to say thank you." The voice had faded out in the ball of flames.

With chagrin, he kept plodding along the muddy ground. The trees seemed to unwelcome the sudden heavy downpour of rain, for some of their leaves fell moodily from the branches. However, the green grasses kissed them with gladness.

A small house snagged his attention, and he neared it. He knocked, and the villager opened the door for him.

"What happened to you, young man?" A gray-haired, older man wearing black clothes asked, his forehead crumpled with confusion.

"An evil she-creature killed my friends," Ferro replied, sniffling. "I would have died if not for the mer—" he paused as he thought of the mermaid's beautiful face, "never mind."

The older man's face scrunched with puzzlement. "Thank God, you're safe. As you can see, the weather is bad, young man. I presume Mother Nature has sympathized with your loss. Get inside and eat, son."

Ferro didn't move.

"I'm Uncle Sammy. Call me Uncle Sam." He smiled. "I'm a good man. Trust me. You're safe here." His authenticity convinced Ferro to get in.

Uncle Sammy prepared dinner for him.

Ferro guzzled a palatable fried chicken and the bread rolls, and his mouth watered.

"The town is enchanting. You shouldn't roam around."

"What do you know about the she-creatures in the river, Uncle Sam?"

"I'd rather not speak. The wind might whisper it to the evil spirits."

"I understand."

"Eat more."

"Thanks."

After he'd eaten, Uncle Sam led him to a small room.

"Pray that the evil will not prosper." Uncle Sammy patted Ferro's shoulders.

"I fear for my life."

"Living in fear is death by default. Living in courage is a march from hell to heaven. So be brave, son."

"Thanks," Ferro said. He lay on a wooden bed, and his weary spirit put him into a deep, dreamless sleep.

After gargling with salt water, Ferro bade farewell to Uncle Sammy, who took good care of him. He likened him to Grandpa Joe, a character in the movie Charlie and the Chocolate Factory that every little boy wished to have for a grandfather. Thanks to his dad, who presented Mr. Joe to him on a couch while melting popcorn in his mouth.

Before he left, Uncle Sammy had given him a pen and advised him to use it during an emergency. Ferro's lips twitched, for the pen was no different from the other writing pens he used in school. He put it in his pocket, anyway.

Ferro tramped to his Granny's house, determined to ask her questions about his past and the she-creatures in the river. It didn't take him long to reach the place. As he was approaching, his Granny stood at the door and embraced him tightly as if it were her last day on Earth.

"Thank God you're alive, dear honey dear!" Mrs. Delphina sobbed, hugging Ferro like a soft pillow.

His Granny's embrace warmed his heart. His tears streamed down his cheeks. They seemed to have minds of their own—they flowed without warning. His eyes were full of questions on which only his granny could shed light.

"Let's get inside. You need some food and rest."

Ferro heaved a deep sigh and steeled himself to blast his M16 rifle of exasperation. "Yeah, you're right. I need that, Granny, but there's far more important things than that. I need answers. Who am I? Who are those freak she-creatures in the river? Why did they know me?"

"My dear honey dear, you rest first, and I'll tell you everything later."

"No, Granny! Please tell me now. Please!" His voice rived, his face sulked, and he gave her a sniff of disapproval.

Mrs. Delphina snuffled in defeat. She whirled around and took something from the drawer. She held a small bottle with multicolored liquid in her hand. "Drink this potion, and everything shall be revealed to you in seconds."

"What's that, Granny? Another potion of oblivion?" Ferro drawled. "If I drink that, I might only forget what happened yesterday, like what you did to me when I was a kid, as told by the wicked she-creature."

"Don't be stubborn, dear. Trust me, this time."

With hesitation, Ferro grabbed the bottle of potion and drank it. As soon as the potion entered into his bloodstream, memories of the past began to flash back like scenes in a television show— his childhood memories with the two she-creatures as they mirthfully swam in the river, their water games, their talks, and laughter as they settled on the rock near the riverside. He called a she-creature with a golden tail Olivia and a black-tailed one, Lucy. He couldn't believe he and the she-creatures were childhood friends—not even when his Granny mixed a potion of oblivion with the orange juice he drank.

"Why did you do that, Granny?" Ferro scowled with an abyss of frustration. "How in the name of heaven have you kept this thing away from me?"

How could my grandmother take away my childhood memories? She was a thief in the night, like Aladdin, who stole the magic lamp from the cave of wonders. Unforgivable act beyond logical comprehension!

"I did it for your own sake. I did it to protect you and our family. If I didn't do it, you wouldn't be standing now before me. Believe me, dear honey dear," explained Mrs. Delphina, her voice shaking. "Forgive me, Ferro."

"I believe in you, Granny, but I'll make my decision this time. I'll seek vengeance for my friends' death," he said with bitterness.

"Listen to me, Ferro. Vengeance is not ours. It's God's. I'm sorry for losing your friends, but the incident didn't happen if they only followed my advice, doing the cross sign before crossing the bridge."

Ferro glowered at his Granny with anguish in his heart. He spun and strode outside the house. He would've treaded to the river when his grandmother followed him.

"If you're already decided about your plan, I think you need this." Mrs. Delphina handed him a shell of a nautilus. Ferro arched his eyebrows as if asking her what he'd do with the shell. "Call her by creating a sound through the shell. Happy birthday, my dear!"

Ferro nodded in gratitude to her. "Yes, it's my birthday today, and I celebrate it with misery. You're forgiven, Granny, even if you didn't ask for it. Thanks for this."

Ferro marched absent-mindedly to the river bridge with the shell in his right hand. He even forgot to make the sign of the cross when crossing the bridge. He sounded the shell when he reached the center. He waited and prepared himself for the things he might see on the river, but nothing was peculiar.

"Olivia!" Ferro shouted. "Where the demon are you? Come out and fight with me."

But Olivia didn't show up.

Ferro would've thrown the shell into the river when a great dabble reverberated. He eagle-eyed on the water, and it was moving. He primed himself. He remembered Uncle Sammy's words about a pen. There was nothing wrong if he tried using it.

He got the pen out of his pocket, and it became a spear. He was startled but held it with all his might.

A woman with a black tail bedazzled him. Ferro gaped and stood immobile. The woman got sapphire-blue eyes ready to mesmerize him, rosy cheeks that would put Snow White to shame, red lips that would make Red Riding Hood's cloak vintage, and her angelic face—sweet and innocent it could erase all the pains of a wounded warrior like him.

Holy fish. Her beauty can end wars and world hunger and stop the glaciers from melting. Right, Ms. Oprah Winfrey?

"Ferro!" She flicked her tail, which brought him back to Earth.

I'm getting swoony here. The way she calls me... uh-oh... it's heaven.

"I–I'm s–s–sorry. I was j–j–just..." Ferro faltered. Lucy's looks fascinated him. *How could a water girl be so gorgeously fair-skinned? If she had a golden tan, I bet she could be the next*

Wonder Woman. Well, there must be something in the waters of Cebu province that made the lady-dwellers devilishly drop-dead gorgeous.

"Put your spear down," she commanded in a silky voice.

I will, my Queen. After all, in a Kingdom of Femme Fatale, you're the queen, and I'm just your king willing to be your servant to do all your bidding. Or beddings? Joke.

"Sure." Ferro dropped his spear, and it returned into a pen. He then took it and put it in his pocket. He also laid the shell of the nautilus. He noticed its hacceity—the capito pedal cartilage, which looked like a wing—and it created soothing music when he accidentally touched it. He rubbed his chin on the weird things beholding him. He gazed at her, and she did the same— their eyes met and spoke of a language only their hearts could understand, for when the speech failed, the eyes triumphed.

She bit her lip as she shifted away from his stares.

It's okay, dude, to blink, or else your eyelashes might get paralyzed. His inner god teased him.

"Hmmm, thank you for saving my life." Ferro broke their silence. He cocked his head and bit his lower lip. "If my memory serves me right, you're Lucy. Correct?"

She bites her lip, and I bite mine. Meeting of the minds or mating of our lips? Holy lips.

"You're welcome," she smiled. "I couldn't afford to see you hurt at Olivia's foolishness. You're my childhood friend. To answer your question, yes, I'm Lucy."

"Thanks again, Lucy. You haven't changed all along. I mean... your attitude. You're still kind, like the old days." *Damn it! You're still beautiful, Luz.*

Lucy grinned while flicking her hair, styled in a teased, low ponytail back over her shoulder. "I believe your granny brought your memories back with you," she said, trying to change the topic, breaking the awkwardness that enveloped them.

"Yeah, you're right, she did. I miss you, Lucy. I do." Ferro's inner god shouted 'whoa'—at long last, the words he held from his aorta escaped from his sinful lips.

Lucy's candy-red-apple blood rushed into her cheeks, and her inner siren shagged.

Ferro espied it. "I mean, I miss our childhood days." *I got you, babe.*

"Yeah, I miss it too." Lucy simpered in a girlish way. "By the way, happy birthday, Ferro."

"Thanks."

"How old are you?"

"Old enough to handle you," Ferro almost whispered it, but Lucy heard it and crooked her eyebrow.

"Excuse me?"

"I mean, I'm seventeen years old."

"You look good at seventeen."

"I look good—"

"Ferro." Lucy stopped him. It was a warning—from his girl— to behave.

"I mean, I look good because of you." He could've said, 'I look good inside you,' but Lucy gave him the I-will-knock-you-down look if he'd voiced out what he thought. In his opinion, Lucy was the real boss—and he was just the CEO—so he must follow the Owner of his heart.

Lucy shook her head. "You were born in a year of abundance. Horses run to and fro in merriment."

"Yeah, Mom told me about it." Ferro agreed with a smile. "I was born on May 1, 2000. The world is lucky enough that a fascinating boy was born. You think so?"

"I couldn't agree more." Lucy bit her lip. "What year is it now?"

"2017," Ferro replied, grinning. "How about you? When were you born?"

"Secret."

"Oh, that's bad, Lucy." Ferro pouted his lips. "Good girls don't say that."

Uh-oh. "I was born—" Lucy paused.

"To love me," Ferro horned in. And he winked at her.

Lucy rolled her eyes. Her inner siren somersaulted.

"Gorgeous. Don't you ever do that again." It was a warning from Mr. Flirty.

"Rolling my eyes? Why not?"

"I'll punish you."

Lucy chuckled. "Punish me." It was not a question.

"Yes, I will."

"What would my punishment be?" Lucy played along with him. She might've gotten an idea of how flirty Ferro was. She might use it against Mr. Dangerously Naughty someday.

"I'll make you roll over the ocean or on my bed. Your choice."

Lucy shook her head, chuckling. "You're unbelievably hilarious... and flirty."

"I am." Ferro winked at her again.

Lucy luminesced a sugary smile. "Want some adventure?"

Ferro answered, "By all means, it's my day, so take me wherever to forever." And he took his shirt off. Lucy couldn't help but gawk at his six-pack abdomen. Her bitchy inner siren exclaimed, "*Magnifico. Pièce de résistance.*"

"Like what you're seeing?" Ferro bit his lip.

Lucy would've rolled her eyes again, but she remembered Ferro's words vividly. Ferro would've unbuttoned his jeans when Lucy halted him.

"What exactly are you doing?" Lucy smirked.

"I'm removing it. We'll have an adventure underneath the river or some water games. I believe it would be good to stay comfortable—" he paused, whispering, "with you."

"Not necessary. You're fine with your jeans on."

"But gorgeous—"

"No buts, or else—"

"You kick my butt?" Ferro winked at her for the third time. Lucy chortled, for she didn't know what to do with the guy in front of her.

"Gorgeous?"

Lucy went red. *How many times will he say that word? It makes me...swoon.* She flung her tail and designed a whirlpool, and a water horse broke out.

"Jump," she instructed.

Flabbergasted, Ferro jumped into the water horse and rode on it. His inner flirty god evaporated. He batted his eyelashes, for he'd never believed he rode again on a horse made of water.

Lucy sank her body into the crystal-clear water and plunged with a flip of her tail. Her figure surfaced, and her tail glistened. She popped her head out and yelled at Ferro.

"Let's race. Let's see who'll reach the Great Rock first!"

"Okay, let the race begin!" Ferro crowed back at her.

The Great Rock was nestled in the middle of the Riverlandia, the ten-kilometer-long river, with whom the people in the village feared because they thought it got lives every year—its accomplice was the bridge.

Lucy swam as fast as she could while Ferro floundered with his horse, which hurtled on the water's surface, but eventually, he got used to it. As the race continued, several creatures like the thumb-size merfairies, the dancing smilaxes, a school of flying fish, and the parrots spurred them on.

Giggles and yells filled the river.

Lucy won the race.

"Just like the old times, boss. You lose," the water horse spoke.

"I know." Ferro chortled while trying to caress the horse's head. "Thanks for the great ride, brother."

"You're welcome, boss. Your servant Liam is always ready to serve you," the horse said. Liam called him boss, while Ferro called him brother. A bond of undeniable friendship between them rekindled like the old times. Liam couldn't forget Ferro's terrified look the first time the young man rode on him during his childhood days.

"Thanks, brother." Ferro tittered at him, and his eyes fixed on Lucy. "Congratulations, as always, you win."

"Thank you. I know someday you'll beat me."

"You think of that? I doubt," he said as he alighted on the Great Rock.

The water horse ceased when Lucy spun her tail. "I bet," she said with a big smile and wallowed beside him.

Silence enveloped them for a minute. Ferro thumped his fingers, moving to Lucy's hand, and their fingers intertwined.

Lucy felt an electric current surge in her veins and took her hand off. It was tingling and electrifying. She might've gotten a heart attack if she didn't take her hand away from his.

But Ferro seemed unstoppable, and this time, he tickled her.

Mr. Doesn't Want Rolling Eyes had many limitless strategies to advance his desires. Lucy thought.

Lucy began to share her fun-filled adventures in the depths of the river and the Crystal Kingdom with Ferro, while Ferro told her about his city life.

"Lucy, you must be tired now," Ferro said seriously.

"No, I'm not. What made you think so?" Lucy asked, her eyebrow raised an inch.

"'Cause you keep running in my mind since the day I met you." Ferro laughed and gave Lucy heart fingers.

Lucy smiled again. Ferro furthered.

"You're a matchstick."

"No, I'm not. But why?"

"You're a matchstick, and so am I. We're a perfect match made in the sky."

Lucy couldn't restrain her laughter. She burst out like a hot balloon. But in a nanosecond, she clasped her hands on her mouth, for her laughs might reach the Crystal Kingdom. *Where on earth did Ferro get all his flirtatiousness?*

"Lucy?"

"Fer?"

"Can you give me your side view?"

Lucy seemed to be mind-controlled by Ferro that she followed every request he'd made from her. "Like this?' She turned sideways.

"Great. Turn your back," Ferro bossed her around. Lucy did. "Perfect."

"Thanks."

"You're great. You're perfect. But something is lacking, Lucy," he said while he playfully craned his eyebrows.

"And what is that?" Lucy smirked again.

Ferro bit his lip. "Me."

Lucy's jaw dropped. Before she got carried away by Ferro's plausible tongue, she'd mused.

"Come, I'll show you the wonders of the river."

"Let the adventure begin, baby." Ferro's excitement increased exponentially that he'd almost forgotten he had a granny waiting for him to celebrate his birthday. After all, he'd come to town to spend quality time with her. *I know you'll understand me, Gran.*

www.ingramcontent.com/pod-product-compliance
Lightning Source LLC
Chambersburg PA
CBHW031459130726
47989CB00003B/1464